Risking it
All for
Love

Yoshihiko Shugo

Sougansha Paperback

Risking it All for Love

First published in Japan in 2013 by Sougansha.
Copyright © Yoshihiko Shugo 2013
Author: Yohihiko Shugo
Translator: Joe Matsui
Illustlator: Yukiko Nagumo

ISBN 978-4-907981-09-9
Sougansha Paperbacks are edited and published by Sougansha, 2-13-14 Fujimachi, Nishi-Tokyo-shi, Tokyo, Japan 202-0014.
shopmaster@sougansha.co.jp

Table
of
contents

Chapter 1

The orders from operational HQ said to wait behind a hill for the target's car to show up. But when I got to the designated place, there was no hill. There was just desert as far as the eye could see.

To give HQ the benefit of the doubt, maybe the "waves" of sand swelling up ahead of me do look like a hill.

In fact, the German panzer unit, that with only five panzers expelled the entire French army brigade stationed here before WW2, called this place "Baguette Hill". It was probably a "German joke" among soldiers weary of looking out over the boring, flat, never-ending North African desert.

The staff at HQ could have come up with the plan without making a proper reconnaissance of the area. They *must have seen "hill" marked on the map and figured it would be a good place to hide. We've got such a lousy HQ, it's no wonder we've been losing so much ground lately to government forces.*

HQ's so incompetent, everything they do strains the troops at the front line. The target would come this way on the straight road passing right next to the "wave." There's nowhere to hide; they'd see us all the way down the road, sitting here totally exposed.

Who'd risk driving straight into an ambush?

Irritated, Nouvat clicked his tongue and lifted his rifle down from his shoulder, shoving the butt end into the sand.

Next to him, Elicia was assembling the combat

emplacement, trying to mount her rifle. Even through her uniform, he could see the voluptuousness of her form as she bent over. Though rather small, she was clearly fully matured as a grown woman. With black hair and brown skin, her face was breathtaking, but still with hints of girlishness. This might have been true of any woman in her early 20s, but with this girl, the incongruity was especially striking.

Somehow Nouvat always felt irritated watching the female soldier's behavior. Maybe it was because she was from the Tata tribe.

"Hey you! What d'you think you're doing setting up the emplacement like that? You want to be nice and let the enemy know we're here?"

Unaware his voice was rising, Nouvat began to sound

belligerent.

"I'm sure HQ's orders said to lie in ambush waiting for the target's car to pass? How could you neutralize a car coming towards us without a combat emplacement? What's that heavy-looking thing sitting on your neck—a hippo's butt?"

Elicia didn't give in easily. In all fairness, it was nearly always like this when a Tata and an Emab had to deal with each other.

"Cut it out, you two," said Colonel Zakarite tersely, standing behind them looking through binoculars.

Obeying Zakarite's command, Nouvat had no choice but to keep his mouth shut. Likewise, Elicia held her tongue.

"The target is expected to pass by in two hours. Till then, we're going to be quiet and wait," said Zakarite bending over and taking a cigar out of the pocket of his uniform. Warming the cigar with a zippo, he lit it, and exhaled smoke with evident satisfaction.

Nouvat likewise lay down quietly, keeping his eyes on the long, straight road that stretched to the horizon.

Sitting next to her emplacement, Elicia also watched the road.

Occasionally, gusts of wind blew eddies of sand into the air all around the desert.

Chapter 2

When the air-conditioner's airflow was full, the engine speed suddenly dropped. However, the car didn't feel much cooler.

Anyhow, the Mercedes is so ancient, it's one we rarely see in Japan. It isn't built for Africa's blazing sun.

In this country, though, even a Toyota Corolla costs 3 million yen because of the 100% customs duties on imported cars. Surely an embassy's official vehicle cannot be a Toyota Corolla or Prius. It looks as though we're going to have to put up with this battered old car for a while.

Kenta Sakurai wiped the beads of sweat formed on his hands by holding the wheel with his shirt, whistling to take his mind off the heat as much as possible. His whistling sounded better than he'd anticipated, and excited, he continued to whistle, putting more emotion into it.

"Mr Sakurai, why don't you stop whistling?"

An irritated voice could be heard from the back.

When Kenta looked in the rear-view mirror, he saw Ambassador Keijiro Akiba sitting in the back seat, glaring at him more fiercely than his voice suggested.

In this ridiculous heat, Ambassador Akiba wore a suit in all seriousness, with his hair sharply parted and wearing a pair of glasses so outdated that no one buys them these days. Kenta reckoned the glasses glinted.

"You don't like music, Ambassador? This is a love song that's very popular in this country just now. It's got passionate lyrics, such as, 'Don't lie to the true feelings in your heart; Make me yours right now,' sung by a band that's really popular among young girls here."

"I don't hate music. I'm just warning a subordinate not to be disrespectful by whistling in front of your superior."

"I understand that you are feeling down, relegated to such a remote place in Africa."

"Don't talk nonsense! I haven't been relegated and I'm not feeling down! One of the pillars of Japanese foreign policy is to deepen friendship with African countries, which is a matter of great importance for our government in gaining a permanent seat on the U.N. Security Council."

"Well, Ambassador. You'd better get used to this remote corner of the continent sooner rather than later, because you've been transferred anyway."

Akiba's huge sigh was audible from the back seat.

"It looks as if getting used to this country is going to be much easier than getting used to you."

Kenta had lived a vagabond life out of Japan, and recently found employment as staff at the Japanese embassy. With such a background, he had a hard time understanding Akiba's feelings.

Akiba is an elite who passed the diplomatic service exam after graduating from the University of Tokyo. Even though he's been transferred to a small country in Africa, he's still an Ambassador. It's a reputable position with a guarantee of pension; he'll have nothing to worry about on his retirement. What on earth can be his reason for being irritated?

Wait, maybe he wants a mistress? This middle-aged man is lonely, in short. Women are my field of expertise. Leave it to me, Ambassador.

Suddenly Kenta became energetic.

"Knowing the local girls is the best way to get used to this country. The girls around here are known for their beauty, even in Africa. So passionate, day and night..."

"What are you talking about? I have family in Japan."

"Don't worry. Nobody cares about them in this country. A family in Japan doesn't exist for the local girls, who think the moon is closer than Japan. You'll find one or two 'local wives' soon enough."

"Shut up!" Akiba raised his voice, losing his patience. "Even if you're local staff, you are a member of the Embassy of Japan after all. Be careful about how you speak and behave so as to uphold Japanese dignity. As Embassy staff, you should always control yourself and put friendship foremost with local people..."

"Holy shit!"

While shouting, Kenta slammed on the brakes with all his might.

The brakes made a sharp noise, and Kenta leaned forward almost hitting the wheel with his chest. He realized that Akiba's head had been thrown against the back of the passenger seat.

"What on earth has just happened?"

Adjusting his shifted glasses, Akiba leaned forward to the side of the driver's seat.

Slowly raising his arm, Kenta pointed forward. He realized his finger was shaking.

"Ambassador, could you please practice the 'friendship with local people' you just talked about, here and now?"

Over the front windshield, a soldier in camouflage armed

with a rifle was approaching with his hand signaling them to stop the engine. Farther away, two soldiers were aiming their way with rifles on gun emplacements.

Chapter 2

Chapter 3

It was just like a terrorists' hideout in a movie set designed by a Hollywood director.

In a small, windowless room, a naked bulb was hanging down from the ceiling. There was a sturdy-looking wooden door in the coarse mud wall, with the wind blowing sand against it making a continuous noise. The dirt floor was covered with the sand that blew in.

In this dreary room, there wasn't even a chair.

Even if Kenta and Akiba hadn't been on the floor with their hands tied behind them, they would have had difficulty in finding a place to sit down.

After their abduction by a trio of armed soldiers, Kenta and Akiba were blindfolded and brought to this hideout. They were thrown into a room and their blindfolds taken off, then their hands were tied and their mouths gagged.

Left on their own, Kenta and Akiba made eye contact many times over, yet they could do nothing. In fact, they might have been able to undo their restraint somehow. However, as the armed group's aim and intent were unknown, if they let themselves loose it could anger the soldiers. In the end, they couldn't help but lie on the floor and do nothing.

After a few hours of neglect, a metallic noise sounded as if the key were turning on the other side of the door, which opened with a squeal.

A short grey-haired man entered the room calmly. He looked to be in his mid-40s. Unlike his military uniform, he had a gentle manner and an intelligent gleam in his eyes.

A hefty man followed with a gun in his hand. He had a searching look and the bottom half of his face was covered in thick beard. He must have been in his 30s.

The soldier who followed the bearded man was surprisingly a female. What was more, she was astonishingly beautiful. While Kenta stared at her unintentionally, she looked back at him. After they looked at each other for some time, she was the first to look away. A tray with something that looked like food was in her hand. Kenta noticed it, and let a sigh of relief escape, realizing they were not going to get killed anytime soon.

As the grey-haired man gave a sharp wave, the bearded man moved behind Kenta and Akiba and removed their gags.

The grey-haired man smiled.

"My name is Zakarite, Colonel of the Revolutionary Alliance of Freedom Fighters. We're very grateful for your cooperation with our Revolutionary Alliance."

He indeed spoke fluent Japanese.

Perhaps because Kenta and Akiba both looked dumbfounded, Zakarite laughed delightedly.

"I studied in Tokyo in my 20s. Tokyo is a superb city. I still dream about the Monja Yaki I had in Tsukishima.[1]"

"Revolutionary Alliance of Freedom Fighters is an anti-government army, isn't it? Did you kidnap us knowing that we're Japanese diplomats?"

Akiba asked in a high-pitched voice failing miserably to

---

1. Monja Yaki is a savory Japanese pancake with various fillings, mostly eaten in the Kanto region. Tsukishima is famous for Monja Street, where visitors find dozens of Monja Yaki restaurants.

sound calm.

"Of course, we knew. We're careful about choosing who to welcome as guests."

"What is your purpose? The Japanese government has expressed neutrality in this country's civil war."

"That's not enough for us. We demand the Japanese government cease funding our government. When our demands are met, you'll be free again."

"So, what happens to us if the request is not fulfilled?"

"It would be a sad end to us, and you two as well."

"WTF. Give me a break!"

Instinctively Kenta stood up shouting. The bearded man promptly hit his shoulder with the gunstock, knocking him to the ground. Kenta groaned with pain. It was as if his shoulder were blown off.

As Kenta lifted his head in pain, his eyes again met the female soldier's. Startled, she immediately looked away.

"Nouvat. Do not hurt our guests."

When Zakarite chided him in French, an official language in this country, the bearded man called Nouvat once again stood at attention.

Again Zakarite ordered the female soldier in French. "Elicia, give them the food."

Elicia reached down to put the tray on the floor in front of Kenta and Akiba. Again, her eyes met Kenta's.

When Kenta tried to smile, she looked away, flustered.

A shy beauty makes an attractive picture. Kenta stared vacantly at Elicia for a while, forgetting the situation he was in.

"May god bless you."

With this, Zakarite left the room. Nouvat and Elicia followed him. Elicia looked back at Kenta before leaving. She closed the door, a little reluctant to leave.

"Ambassador, we're in a pretty serious situation, aren't we?" Kenta spoke with a sigh.

"When this happens, it's best to sit still and wait to avoid irritating them."

"So it looks as if our lives depend on the Japanese government's bargaining power now. Doesn't that seem a bit hopeless?"

"There is hope, Mr Sakurai. Our lives depend on YOU."

"Pardon?"

Kenta looked at Akiba's face in spite of himself.

Akiba was nodding with self-confidence.

Chapter 4

In the temporary barracks next to the hideout, Nouvat and Elicia were glaring at each other over coffee that'd been cold for some time.

Zakarite was in the armchair puffing a cigar, not giving a damn about them at all.

"Why the fuck am I not fit to be a soldier? You'd better take that back."

The veins stood out on her forehead; her lips trembled with rage.

This face, this impudence makes me detest her. Nouvat couldn't help feeling sick.

"The revolution isn't leisure. You lot will rot our army for sure."

"Is this about the grudge you had this morning? We caught the targets in the end, didn't we?"

"That's not what I'm talk'n 'bout! You are not a soldier if you put yourself before discipline. That's what I'm saying!"

"When the hell did I put myself before discipline?"

"Your eyes tell me everything. I can see it as clear as day. I'm not blind."

"Wha', what do you mean?"

"You were looking at the young Japanese hostage, weren't you? He was such a tasty lookin' boy."

"No, I was just keeping a watch..."

Elicia seems to be getting restless, so I must have nailed it.

"Damn. That's why I hate country bumpkins like the Tata tribe," Nouvat spat out. Suddenly Elicia's face changed color.

"What did you say? I'm not going to let you talk that way about our tribe!"

Elicia stood up and pulled out a gun, thrusting it under Nouvat's nose.

Nouvat instinctively grabbed his gun and aimed at Elicia.

"You two, don't do anything stupid!" Zakarite shouted sharply.

Hearing this dignified voice permitting no objection, both Nouvat and Elicia reluctantly lowered their guns.

Zakarite stood up slowly.

"Tribal feuding is a chronic disease throughout Africa. No true revolution can be achieved without overcoming such an obstacle. We must all cooperate as comrades aiming at revolution, regardless of the tribe we come from. Do you understand, Nouvat?"

"Yes, Colonel."

"These hostages are our precious trump card to make an appeal to the international community. You should keep this in mind, Elicia," Zakarite emphasized.

"Yes, Sir," Elicia nodded obediently.

"For the sake of revolution, keep your desires to yourself. OK, Elicia?"

"I know."

"If you ever touch our hostages, I'll kill you. Remember that!" Nouvat pointed his forefinger at Elicia.

Elicia hurriedly left the room, quietly biting her bottom lip.

She slammed the door shut.

"Huh! What a barbarian!"

"Nouvat! Shut your mouth."

Feeling ticked off by Zakarite, Nouvat couldn't help but keep quiet.

He sat down and picked up his mug.

Someone behind him patted him on the back. When Nouvat looked back, he saw Zakarite nodding and looking at him with a gentle expression and returning to his armchair.

It was as if he was telling Nouvat that he knew how deeply Nouvat cared about the army.

I'm no match for this Colonel.

Nouvat sipped the cold coffee from his mug, shrugging with a wry smile.

Chapter 5

"Do you want me to flirt with that female soldier?"

It's pitiful. The voice coming out of my mouth sounds so silly.

Has this guy scared himself into madness?

While Kenta looked puzzled, Akiba nodded, pretending to be full of confidence.

"Listen. The current ruling party avoids trouble at all costs. They are hopeless in negotiating hostage releases. We've got to try to help ourselves."

"I can see that, but isn't it a bit of a long shot to flirt with a woman? Also, wouldn't it make things worse if I fail?"

"It will be OK. Her eyes tell me that she fell in love with you at first sight. You should certainly be able to hit on her."

"But Ambassador, what about the dignity of the Japanese people and controlling myself as a member of embassy staff?"

"We don't have the luxury of doing everything by the book. I'm giving you an order as your Ambassador. Seduce her any way you can!"

Akiba's loud voice reverberated in the room.

"Yes, Ambassador..."

To tell the truth, I can't understand what this elite guy, this University of Tokyo graduate, is thinking. Isn't the appropriate course of action for a high-ranking official such as an Ambassador to quietly wait the results of government negotiation, rather than gambling on a reckless plan?

While Kenta was puzzled, Akiba leaned forward in excitement.

"I am not meant to die in a place like this. I got posted to such a small African country because I got mixed up in the current ruling party's fractional conflicts, but if the change of government is successful in the next election, my rehabilitation is quite possible. I could be an Ambassador in a major European country at least, and hopefully back to the center of the Ministry of Foreign Affairs."

"That might be your situation, but I have nothing to do with it."

"Well, how about promoting you as official staff of the Ministry, if we can find our way out of the difficulty? I'm sure it is not so easy to live on your current salary."

Certainly, the local staffs at diplomatic establishments abroad aren't treated as civil servants, so I won't receive a family allowance, retirement allowance, nor transportation expenses, not to mention a welfare pension. The contract is renewable every two years; there is no guarantee of status. Surely my life would be more stable and I wouldn't have to be concerned about life in retirement.

"But this way of life suits my taste, so..."

"What about women?"

"Huh?"

Hearing these unexpected words, Kenta stopped, gaping.

"As an official of the Ministry of Foreign Affairs, you'll be very much in demand by the rich graduates of famous women's universities such as Seishin, Ferris, and Shirayuri. I can introduce you to some of them, if you wish. At receptions, beautiful blondes would be biting every time you cast out a line, like hungry fish. HAHAHA."

There was no longer dignity or self-control in Akiba's expression.

However, the contemptible offer stuck right into the heart

of simple-minded Kenta.

"Ah, are you sure? I'll do it. I'll show you that I can!"

"Good. You can do it."

They would have rejoiced together hand in hand if their hands hadn't been tied at their backs. Laughing frivolously was the best they could do

Then, with a metallic clank sounding from outside the room, the door opened.

Elicia came in and picked up their empty trays.

Akiba winked to signal Kenta.

Kenta struggled for dear life to talk to the female soldier in French.

"How does someone as beautiful as you come to be here with the rebels?"

Elicia glanced at Kenta, but soon turned away and started walking.

Akiba kicked Kenta's foot.

Give me a break, old man. I'm doing my best here.

Kenta begged Elicia to stop.

"Please wait. My name is Kenta. Tell me your name, please."

I already knew her name as Zakarite had called it out, but it would not be a good idea to call her by name before she gave it to me herself. Also, it'll be hopeless if she won't introduce herself to me. Please, answer me!

Elicia contemplated Kenta.

"I'm Elicia."

No sooner said than she turned on her heel and went out of the room.

The door made a metallic sound as the key turned.

I did it! Inside, Kenta clenched his fists in triumph.

Though our communication lasted only a few seconds, it

was big progress.

"Good. Well done, Mr Sakurai. It went well for an initial contact."

Though being talked to by Akiba, Kenta did not look back.

"Elicia. How cute..."

Looking at the door, Kenta couldn't help breaking into a lewd smile.

"Mr Sakurai. This is not a play. Our lives depend on it. You've got to take this more seriously!"

"I know, I know."

Kenta leaned back against the wall, pouting.

Kenta hoped to sleep thinking of Elicia's face tonight.

Chapter 5

Chapter 6

The next afternoon, Zakarite and Nouvat came to the room.

Nouvat stood behind Zakarite with the gun in his hand.

Zakarite cheerfully started telling how negotiations had gone with the Japanese government as if it were the funniest story in the world.

"You see, we didn't waste any time. I called the Japanese Embassy and told the lady who picked up the phone that we had abducted you two, but alas I was told that unfortunately she wasn't able to comment on important matters because the person in charge was absent."

"Who the hell hired that stupid secretary? You all should know it's more than important when the person in charge is absent and unreachable."

Akiba hopelessly looked up at the ceiling.

Zakarite simply continued:

"So, we tried the Ministry of Foreign Affairs in Tokyo to declare what we'd done. Guess what we got—the automatic voice message. The voice said to press seven if the call was regarding diplomatic establishments abroad. We pressed number seven, then we heard the person in charge was on a business trip and they'd get back to us a few days later."

"The Africa division lacks both money and personnel. If we wait here as hostages, I could be long dead of old age when the person in charge finally shows up."

Akiba moaned, writhing.

Zakarite looked sympathetically at Akiba.

"We felt we had no other alternative so we phoned the Prime Minister's official residence. We were told to write; write the declaration and send it to them via either email or FAX. We did so immediately and emailed it. We got an instant reply saying they would make every effort to deliver the information as promptly as possible but it might take a while. In case of urgency, it says, we should contact the relevant department directly by phone. I had a really bad feeling, but I dialed the number anyway."

Listening to their conversation, Kenta began to have a bad feeling about how things would wind up.

Zakarite sighed deeply.

"It was the same person who answered when I pressed seven calling the Ministry of Foreign Affairs."

"No!" Akiba shut his eyes.

"Useless!" Kenta cried.

"I really don't understand. Japan is such a hardworking and brilliant nation and yet its government offices are so inefficient. What a mysterious country. It reminded me of the mysterious taste of Yomogi dango in Shibamata.[2] All we can do now is to wait for the Japanese government to contact us. I am afraid your stay here could be longer than expected."

Zakarite gave them the news and closed the door.

---

2. Mugwort-flavoured rice dumplings, especially popular among visitors to Shibamata Taisyakuten temple.

Kenta and Akiba saw each other but didn't have the willpower to talk. They could only sigh.

Chapter 7

The door opened again. Elicia was bringing dinner.

There was plenty of food on the tray. The quality and quantity were incomparably improved from the previous day. It was clearly a positive sign.

"Eat well." She put the tray in front of Kenta.

That should mean Elicia is getting off guard, shouldn't it?

Kenta felt his heart leap.

Akiba made a lot of coughing sounds. He must have given up on the Japanese government. It seemed he could not be bothered to try hard enough to hide his signal.

Kenta looked into Elicia's eyes.

"Elicia, I am interested in you. Would you tell me more about yourself?"

"Me … I'm …"

A look of bewilderment came over Elicia's face. As she looked at Kenta, her expression grew sad and sentimental.

Kenta felt his heart beat quickly and loudly.

"Elicia. My heart has belonged to you since we first met."

Elicia looked a little startled.

The wonder is that I can say embarrassingly swanky lines in French when I can't possibly in Japanese.

"You and I met here. It is fate. You are my soul mate."

"Fate? Soul mate?"

"Yes. God led us to each other."

Elicia's eyes sparkled.

Good, it's working!

Kenta was excited.

"Elicia, I love you."

Kenta leaned forward.

Elicia also drew closer.

Suddenly the door opened.

"Oi, how long do you need to deliver food?"

The bearded guy called Nouvat entered the room holding the pistol in his hand.

As Elicia quickly stepped aside, Kenta, leaning forward unstably, lost balance and collapsed to the floor. His mouth filled with sand.

"Elicia. What the hell were you doing?"

"Nothing. I was just checking the handcuffs while I happened to be here with a dinner tray."

"Sure you were."

Nouvat turned a doubtful gaze on Elicia and Kenta.

Elicia lowered her eyes biting her lip.

Oh no Elicia. Don't get so shook up, otherwise he'll be even more suspicious!

Kenta twisted his body to sit up again and spat out the sand.

Nouvat grinned.

"OK, how about this? I'll deliver the food to these hostages from now on. You'll be on guard outside."

Elicia opened her eyes wide in resentment.

"Wh, why? Are you saying I cannot even take care of meals

for hostages? Don't look down on me!"

"Whoa, don't you always complain about being treated as a woman? You could thank me for leaving you to the task of guarding the hideout so you can prove you are an excellent soldier. I'll take on the trivial work, like delivering meals to the hostages."

Elicia was at a loss for words. There appeared to be no way she could bring forward a counterargument.

So was Kenta. It was not a hostess bar; there was no such thing as caregiver nomination system for hostages. If Kenta insisted on letting Elicia bring meals, it would surely raise suspicion about their plans.

Elicia turned her back on him quietly and walked out of the

room with quick steps.

Nouvat looked down on Kenta with a half smile.

"Don't look so sad, man. I helped you here."

With these words, Nouvat also left the room giving a playful salute.

Kenta felt as if he was losing all his strength.

"Ambassador, I can't see Elicia anymore."

"I know," Akiba concurred, making a vinegary face. "Did he just say he helped you?"

"What about it?"

"Don't you find it strange? How come changing the caregiver means helping you?"

"That is strange, actually."

"Ultimately, our plans could all have been leaked to them already, couldn't they? Was it a warning to us knowing what we are planning to escape?"

"I see. Our lives are guaranteed as long as we obey. But if we try to escape with Elicia's help, they can't help but kill us … Is that what you are saying?"

"Yes, so I think he was saying that he helped us by preventing us from committing to an escape plan, which is already known."

"But, how did they know our plans? We were by ourselves in this room, not to mention speaking Japanese."

"There must be a wiretap. It's a common practice in international politics. Besides, the Colonel speaks Japanese very well."

"So, we have no options left, then."

"Uh huh …"

Akiba moaned and stopped talking. He appeared lost in thought.

Kenta worried about the possibility that he would not see Elicia again, more than the fact that the escape plan had broken down.

"Elicia …"

Kenta muttered, his mouth full of sand.

Chapter 8

The next day, Nouvat delivered the meals, breakfast followed by lunch.

The food was shabby again, just like before.

Rather than moaning about the worsening food, Kenta was more anguished by the fact that he could no longer see Elicia.

After lunch, it was Nouvat again who came in to take the tray away.

"Hey man, you look so down."

Nouvat simpered, teasing Kenta.

"No, I don't."

His blunt reply was eloquent proof of his lack of spirit.

"Excuse me, are you Mr Nouvat?"

Suddenly Akiba spoke cheerfully to Nouvat.

"What's up, Mr Ambassador?"

"Maybe it's not our business as outsiders, but isn't there something wrong with the relationships among the anti-government rank and file?"

"Everything is ok, thank you."

Nouvat made a sour face.

"Emab tribesmen occupy almost all the important posts

in the government while the anti-government forces are groups of minority tribes. Rumor says the Emab in the anti-government forces avoid fighting the Emab in the government army."

"That's nonsense! I'm an Emab. Yet I have always led charges into enemy lines and killed more government dogs than anyone. Do you know why?"

"For the cause of revolution?"

"I don't believe in a revolution. I believe in Colonel Zakarite. If he says a revolution is necessary, I'll sacrifice myself for it. If he says I have to make friends with other tribes, I'll obey his orders. It's as simple as that."

"Nonetheless, you didn't look as though you were getting

along well with that female soldier?"

"Tatas, especially impertinent women, are exceptions. Of course, I won't do anything to embarrass the Colonel. But I'll never, ever let my guard down against the Tatas."

"Are the Tatas such a terrifying tribe?"

"No, not terrifying. But, they are so rustic and savage and would never try to mingle with other tribes. Their customs are so different from ours. I can't fight alongside them. Foreigners like you might not have heard about it, but Tatas are traditionally…"

"I don't know much about the problems of the Tata tribe," Akiba interrupted Nouvat's criticisms of Tatas. "However, I do have certain information about the crisis within the rebel forces."

"What?"

Nouvat's expression changed completely.

"I was actually at the center of the Ministry of Foreign Affairs in Japan before being transferred to this country. Among the information made available to me, there was some about the government army and anti-government forces, as well as intelligence supplied by the CIA. Have you noticed there is a covert movement in progress to exclude the Emabs from the anti-government forces? That is why the Japanese government is doubtful of the ability of the rebels to continue war, and so they're maintaining neutrality."

"Exclusion of the Emabs? Are you sure?"

"Honestly, I cannot guarantee the credibility of such information. But you won't lose anything by knowing something."

"Just say it."

"I want to talk to your boss directly. In a room without wiretaps."

Nouvat looked dubious for a moment, but soon headed for the door.

"Wait a minute. I'll check the Colonel's schedule," Nouvat said turning back, then left the room.

Kenta brought his face closer to Akiba.

"Ambassador, that's astonishing information. Just as might be expected of an elite Ministry of Foreign Affairs official. If things go well, it wouldn't be impossible to demand our release in exchange of the information …"

"Don't forget about wiretaps! Speak in a low voice," Akiba whispered into Kenta's ear.

"Ok, ok," Kenta lowered his voice too. "You know, if things go well, we can negotiate our release in exchange of the information."

"It's a lie."

"Huh?"

"You should know that talk was a line. The Japanese

government does not have much of a unique ability to gather intelligence, and the MoFA's Africa Department is simply to welcome guests when politicians visit Africa. Did you really think the CIA would give the department confidential information?"

"So, what was that talk for … ?"

"When I meet Colonel Zakarite in a separate room, that Nouvat will definitely be there as a guard."

"Ah!" Kenta cried out unintentionally.

"Keep your voice down!"

After reproaching Kenta, Akiba gave an affirmative nod.

Akiba brought his mouth closer to Kenta's ear again.

"Listen. I'm going to buy as much time as possible during the meeting with Zakarite, telling as many lies as possible. It will be Elicia who brings dinner to you. And there won't be anyone left to listen to your conversation through a wiretap. Mr Sakurai, you've got to seize the opportunity to approach Elicia. This could be our last chance. Stake your life on winning her heart."

"Ambassador, …"

Kenta stared at Akiba quietly.

"I understand. Watch me, I'll win her over, whatever it takes!"

Unconsciously Kenta raised his voice close to Akiba's ears.

"Well, maybe I should worry more about my ears than my life."

Akiba smiled wryly.

A metallic sound echoed outside, and the door opened.

"Colonel Zakarite requires your presence. Ambassador Akiba only."

Standing up with Nouvat's support, Akiba mouthed "Counting on you" before going out of the room.

Chapter 9

As Akiba correctly predicted, it was Elicia who came in with the dinner in her hand.

It looked as though Nouvat had given her a strict warning. Elicia put the tray down in a distant manner, and headed for the door without a glance at Kenta.

In desperation, Kenta called her to stop.

"Elicia. Please wait!"

Elicia stopped for a second but touched the door still not looking at Kenta.

"Elicia. Do you believe in fate? I do. I want to believe it."

Elicia stopped. "I ... I want to believe in fate, too," she

muttered without looking back.

Kenta's internal organs undulated simultaneously. Elicia's feelings are moving slowly but surely!

"I'd wandered around the world looking for my soul mate. I've dated many girls. But the moment I met you, passion began swelling up from the bottom of my heart."

Elicia turned back. "Really?"

"I'm sure. It's fate that we met here."

"Kenta, are you my 'soul mate'?"

"I am. I am your 'soul mate' and I'm all yours."

Elicia covered her face with her hands.

"Kenta is mine … Would god allow this?"

An agonized look came over Elicia's face.

Innocence like this is long gone in Japan, or in any developed country.

Kenta's heart filled with affection for Elicia.

"I came from a country far, far away. But, why would god let me meet you Elicia, if he doesn't allow it?"

"I don't know. I really don't know what to do."

"Elicia, I love you."

"Kenta … No … No, I can't!"

Vehemently shaking her head, Elicia turned and ran out of the room through the door.

"Elicia!"

Kenta's cry reverberated in the vacant room.

Chapter 10

"How many divisions are involved in the plot to exclude the Emab tribe?"

"What is a 'division'?"

"A division in our country consists of 9,000 soldiers in peace time, which expands to a little under 30,000 in war time."

"Aha. So, the organized strength is different in times of peace and war?"

"This organization is modeled after the Japanese army before World War II. How is it that a diplomat from Japan doesn't have such basic military knowledge?"

Though Zakarite gave him an astonished look, Akiba was only smiling.

Nouvat could not believe what was happening in front of him was real.

Speaking of being a diplomat, I was thinking it is an occupation for the elite of elites with the highest educational background and cultural level. Japan is after all the country that prides itself on having the best technology and political stability among developed countries.

How is it that country's Ambassador doesn't know the difference between the numbers of soldiers in standing and mobilized armies?

Nouvat couldn't help but wonder why such a pathetic Japanese Ambassador would request a meeting with Colonel Zakarite.

Though he may be a fool, it wouldn't have come out if he were keeping quiet…

At that moment, something flashed into Nouvat's mind.

Is it possible that this innocent-looking diplomat is actually trying to create a diversion?

If his plan were to prevent Colonel Zakarite from leaving this room… and he calculated that I would be on the Colonel's guard…

Nouvat shouted. "Colonel! Cancel this meeting now."

Zakarite looked at Nouvat dubiously.

"If necessary I'll arrange the meeting again some other time.

Please believe my hunch for now and cancel this meeting immediately."

"OK. Ambassador Akiba, I'll certainly make up for this discourtesy later."

Zakarite was known as one of the best commanders in Africa for his promptness in making decisions.

Grabbing Akiba by the lapels and dragging him, Nouvat headed for the hostage's room in a hurry.

Chapter 10

Chapter 11

When Elicia ran out of the hideout, it was dusk.

An immense sun was setting on the endless desert horizon, coloring its surroundings red.

Elicia watched the setting sun, sitting on a tire that was left untouched.

Her heart was still beating fast.

"Kenta…"

Muttering to herself, she instinctively held her breath. Her face flushed, realizing that this would be improper behavior.

"Non, non!"

Scolding herself, Elicia shook her head hard.

She could tell that the hot blood running through her was rushing beyond her control.

He's just a man, and what's more, we just met. Would it be possible to be attracted to such a man? What can I call this emotion?

In fact, Elicia knew what it was.

This is the blood of the Tatas. This is the desire of the Tatas. Once I want something, I cannot stop wanting it.

Among the Tata tribe, it was thought natural for a human to have such a desire.

My father and mother, grandfathers and grandmothers, and great-grandfathers and great-grandmothers, generations of my tribe led us to prosperity by facing their desires honestly.

However, in her teens, the desire growing inside Elicia felt disgusting and detestable, because of the fastidiousness so characteristic of her generation.

Since she'd thrown herself into the revolution, she'd had no leisure to worry about such things in the daily fight. Fighting against the government army, killing enemy soldiers, watching friends die and surviving the civil war was what she devoted all her energies to. She thought she could part from disgusting desires. She believed that reason could overcome passion.

However, the moment she saw the young Japanese among the abducted hostages, her reason crumbled away all too quickly. Her pulse refused to stop racing and sensations welled up inside her.

I don't understand why. I wonder what's happening to me. I scolded myself many times. It simply didn't work.

I want Kenta.

I can't hold back.

Moreover, Kenta said it himself just now. Kenta's mine. He said that god let him meet a soul mate – me.

But…

Elicia's passionate thoughts didn't go further.

If I act purely based on my emotions, it is evident that I would be in breach of military discipline. In a military organization, it is not permissible to give personal emotion priority.

If I touch an important hostage, people will get angry, not only Nouvat. Colonel Zakarite would never forgive me.

If I choose Kenta, it would mean I desert the rebels. Is that a choice I should make?

"Somebody tell me what to do!"

Before she knew it, Elicia was crying out at the setting sun.

Chapter 12

Akiba returned to the room earlier than expected.

Nouvat, his eyes bloodshot, dragged Akiba along asking frantically, "Where's Elicia?"

It would be no good asking Nouvat for relationship counselling. Kenta ignored Nouvat with a forced smile.

When Nouvat left, Akiba drew closer to Kenta as if he couldn't wait any longer.

"Oh dear, it wasn't easy to keep lying. I couldn't help faltering when questioned. Well, I managed to laugh it off somehow."

"I see," Kenta replied helplessly.

"Mr Sakurai, so what happened on your side? Were you able

to have a good chat with Elicia?"

"I believe we understood one another. I need one more push."

"We don't have time for that, Mr Sakurai. I told you this is our last chance."

Last chance … so I cannot see her again?

Just at that moment, Kenta lost all restraint.

"Please buy us some more time, just once more. Let me see Elicia again!"

Kenta pressed Akiba. He was beyond all sense of shame. Seeing Elicia again was all he wanted to do.

"Next time, I'll definitely persuade her. Please keep Nouvat and Zakarite away from this room anyhow."

"That's not possible. I don't have any more tricks."

"How about becoming ill? If pretending illness doesn't work, I can still break your arm so that ..."

"Wait, Mr Sakurai. Calm down, and let's think of something more practical, OK?"

Akiba wore an intensely fearful expression thinking Kenta had gone mad.

Chapter 13

Basking in the glow of the sunset, Elicia kept her eyes downcast.

She couldn't move, torn between emotion and reason.

Heuuuu heuuuu, heuuuww… Piii piii pipiiii …

Elicia raised her head.

A familiar melody sounded from somewhere close.

It was a whistle. It appeared it was coming from the room where the hostages were kept.

"Kenta…"

Murmuring, Elicia stood up like a sleepwalker.

Chapter 14

In the dreary room, the sounds of Kenta's whistles were echoing. The more emotion he put into it, the livelier the song became.

Akiba cautiously started a conversation.

"Are you OK, Mr Sakurai?"

"I know you don't like my whistles. I'm afraid I cannot stop."

"Well, that's not a problem. I just wanted to know, why are you whistling now? Whose song is it?"

"As I told you before, this is a love song that's very popular in this country just now. I am putting my affection for Elicia into this melody. As long as I can't see her in person, this is the only way I can possibly express what I feel."

Replying impatiently, Kenta resumed whistling again.

"Courting through a song? Are you a wild bird?"

Akiba was utterly amazed.

Suddenly the sound of unlocking could be heard. This time, it was unusually muted.

Then the door opened quietly.

Eyes watchful, Elicia entered the room.

Is this a dream?

"Elicia!" Kenta shouted.

"Quiet!"

Elicia put her forefinger to her lips.

"I heard your whistles."

When Kenta nodded, Elicia went round and freed his hands.

While Kenta gently turned his hands after being tied for so long, Elicia freed Akiba of his shackles.

"Elicia, I love you."

When Kenta held Elicia's hands, she returned his gaze with watery eyes.

Ah, this isn't a dream!

Their faces gradually drew near. Elicia opened her lips a little. Kenta moved ahead to kiss her lips passionately…

"Would you mind kissing each other later when we get out of here?"

Akiba intervened in a low voice.

Kenta came to his senses. "Elicia, let's run away, together."

Elicia drew a knife from her waist belt.

"Follow me."

After saying so, she peeked out through the door and went

out.

Kenta and Akiba followed her.

In the hollow corner in the middle of a narrow corridor, the three hid themselves for the time being.

Elicia was seeing how the land lies outside frequently. It looked as if the exit was not so far.

Hiding in the corner himself, Akiba addressed Kenta, his voice filled with excitement.

"Didn't I tell you? I played it cool and my strategy worked."

Kenta turned toward Akiba and whispered.

"Ambassador, I have a favor to ask of you."

"What, you're trying to raise the stakes on the brink of our escape?"

"I can only speak of this at a time like this."

When Kenta urged him on emphatically, Akiba exhaled lightly.

"Well, I've got no choice. Say it."

"If we succeed in getting away, please let me take Elicia to Japan."

"Allow a member of the armed guerillas to enter Japan? No way."

Akiba shook his head.

"Though we can escape now, if she stays in this country, she could be held responsible and executed by the anti-government forces."

"That can't be helped. It's their problem, not mine."

"I beg you!" Kenta touched the sandy floor with his forehead. "You can forget about the promotion as MoFA official staff and the introduction to girls. I'm happy as long as I can start a new life in Japan with Elicia."

"Are you serious? There are women in abundance."

"There's no one like Elicia."

After a short silence, Akiba smiled wryly with a big sigh.

"This is exactly why I don't understand the local staff entirely. Whatever. I'll take responsibility for asking the government to let her in."

"Thank you very much!"

"Quiet!"

Elicia shut the two up with an angry look.

"Never get separated from me, ok?"

A drawn knife in her hand, Elicia moved to the other side of the corridor carefully, then opened the door in one swift movement.

They breathed in the characteristic smell of the desert.

Forming a group, Elicia jumped out into the desert night, followed by Kenta and Akiba.

Chapter 15

Back in the small room where the Japanese hostages were kept, Nouvat and Zakarite were stunned.

The vacant room was all the more dreary with two pairs of shackles and empty dishes left behind on a tray. The hostages had vanished into thin air.

"That bitch!"

"Nouvat, it's too early to judge what happened here."

"It can't be anyone else's doing but Elicia's!"

Finding himself contradicted by Nouvat who rarely turned on him red and angry like this, Zakarite didn't dare rebuke him further.

"In the end, she couldn't control her desire …" Zakarite muttered moaningly.

"Just as I told you. You can't trust country bumpkins like the Tatas."

Nouvat kicked the tray hard. The empty dishes scattered, clattering around the floor.

"Savages like the Tatas never restrain themselves! After all, they've been cannibals for centuries," Nouvat spat out.

He sighed in spite of himself.

"I feel sorry for those Japanese," Zakarite muttered.

"We tried to keep Elicia away from the hostages. We

couldn't help them."

Nouvat shook his head helplessly, breathing out a big sigh.

Chapter 16

The stars twinkled in the sky. Once in a while sparks flew from the campsite, mingling with the stars.

Looking up at the sky, Elicia smiled with satisfaction.

After all, my blood is Tata.

I had no idea what a pleasure it would be to follow such deep desires.

Though other tribes often misunderstand us, we Tatas don't consume human flesh without a second thought. Cannibalism is a sacred ritual to absorb the spirit of the eaten. Naturally, one chooses whom to eat very carefully – the one whose flesh is eaten has to be worthy of such a sacred ritual.

In the past, the Tata warriors are the body of their brave adversaries after battle, with awe and respect for the worthy opponent. Even after the days of wars have passed, amongst us Tatas, it is still considered the greatest blessing in a lifetime to find a person worthy of cannibalism. We call such a person our 'soul mate'.

Of course, one has to ask permission from god to choose a soul mate. However, permission is not so easy to obtain.

The easiest way is that the "soul mate" surrenders himself, expressing god's permission. In this case, the person can be approved to be the soul mate without much trouble, because it is unthinkable for the person to be eaten to lie about god's will.

However, it would be such a rare case. Except for a few

cases in which relatives wish to sacrifice themselves to help a sick child, it is rare to find someone who is willing to be eaten.

In most cases, the oracle tells god's will through tribal elders. However, the oracle is also rarely given. Such a sacred ritual as cannibalism is not simple as other tribes think. A thoughtless man like Nouvat would never understand the subtleties.

The encounter with Kenta was nothing short of destiny. At the first glance, the desire to eat this person swelled up from the bottom of my being. I have never been so conscious of the blood of the Tatas running inside me. It was so difficult to suppress my desire every time our eyes met. I couldn't conceal my consternation when Nouvat pointed out the way I gazed at Kenta.

Preparing to eat them if given the chance, I gave the hostages better food at my own discretion to fatten them up as much as I could.

However, as long as there was no oracle from god, there was no ground to believe this foreigner from the Far East was my soul mate. Up until this point, my reason could suppress my desire.

However, when I realized that god would allow me to have Kenta (He said so himself. There can be no more reliable oracle than this), a hole was pierced in the walls of reason that had contained my desire till then.

Furthermore, the whistles… "Don't lie to the true feelings in your heart; Make me yours right now" *… It blew away what little shred of reason remained in me.*

I am completely liberated from the military, revolution, and even social customs. From now on, I will live freely, as one descended from the proudest Tatas!

Elicia threw the scattered clothes and underwear that belonged to the Japanese into the fire. Sparks rose higher into the air.

Licking the blood-soaked blade of her knife, she gave a loud belch.

Elicia warned herself of one thing after rubbing her full tummy. One can learn a lesson from anything.

Today's lesson:

eat in moderation.

The meat of a haggard old man doesn't taste so good.